DEVOTION

DEVOTION

PATTI SMITH

THE 2016 WINDHAM-CAMPBELL LECTURE

YALE UNIVERSITY PRESS
NEW HAVEN AND LONDON

The *Why I Write* series is published
with assistance from the Windham-
Campbell Literature Prizes, which
are administered by the Beinecke Rare
Book and Manuscript Library at
Yale University.

Yale University Press books may be
purchased in quantity for educational,
business, or promotional use.
For information, please e-mail
sales.press@yale.edu (U.S. office) or
sales@yaleup.co.uk (U.K. office).

Printed in the United States
of America.

Library of Congress Control
Number: 2017933005
ISBN 978-0-300-21862-6
(hardcover : alk. paper)
ISBN 978-0-300-24022-1 (pbk)

A catalogue record for this book is
available from the British Library.

This paper meets the requirements
of ANSI/NISO Z39.48-1992
(Permanence of Paper).

10 9 8 7 6 5

To Betsy Lerner —
my friend and guide

CONTENTS

DEVOTION

Inspiration is the unforeseen quantity, the muse that assails at the hidden hour. The arrows fly and one is unaware of being struck, and that a host of unrelated catalysts have joined clandestinely to form a system of its own, rendering one with the vibrations of an incurable disease — a burning imagination — at once unholy and divine.

What is to be done with the resulting impulses, these nerve endings flickering like an illuminated map of thieving constellations? The stars pulse. The muse seeks to be vivified. But the mind is also the muse. It seeks to outsmart its glorious opponents, to rewire such sources of inspiration. A crystal stream suddenly dried. A thing of beauty joyless, defiled. Why does the creative spirit turn on itself? Why does the maker twist all drama? The pen is lifted, guided by the shattered muse. Without discord, it marks, harmony passes unnoticed, without discord, it continues, Abel is rendered no more than a forgotten shepherd.

How the Mind Works

WRITING DESK, NEW YORK CITY

1

Somehow, searching for something else, I stumbled upon a trailer of a film called *Risttuules,* translated as *In the Crosswind.* It is Martti Helde's requiem for thousands of Estonians who suffered mass deportation to Siberian collective farms in the spring of 1941, when Stalin's troops rounded them up, separated families, and herded them into cattle cars. Death and exile, their fate reassigned.

The filmmaker created a visual poem through a unique dramatization of actors winding through a set of stationary human tableaus. Time suspends yet rushes, spreading images in the form of words drawn from this sad pageant. A terrible gift, I acknowledge as I write, straining to get the words down. Yet even so, I sense that behind them something else is brewing. I follow a mental line and come upon a forest of firs and a pond and a small clapboard house. This was the beginning of that something else, but I didn't know it then.

A winter sketch. Just a road away. A blue dressing gown is a curtain for a window that no one will see through again. There is blood everywhere, drained of its blood color, and a dog barking and stars dropping through pallid skies.

A dying calf. A splint upon the hoof—smears, holes. Night falls, obscuring the twitching limb of the last living thing.

A sketch on time. Gears, small hands in ice suspend. Birds no longer curious cease to wing. The dance is over and the face of love is nothing but the wide skirt and burnished heels of winter.

In the morning I awake with the black-and-white dioramas of *Risttuules* still in my mind, the strained tempo of the human opera embodied in bowed and breathing statues. So taken by its expressive power I cannot recall the objective of my original search. I lay there replaying a slow pan of the banished human chain winding through a relentless flurry of white petals. Chrysanthemums. Yes! Branches of them and the wretched train of life blurring past. Yet returning to the same bit of film I had viewed earlier, I find no such scene. Had I unwittingly projected it? I push aside my computer and cast a ruling upon the uneven plaster ceiling: we pillage, we embrace, we know not. I get up to urinate. I imagine snow.

With the delicate voice of Erma, the female narrator of *Risttuules,* fresh in my ear, I dress, grab my notebook and a copy of Patrick Modiano's *Paris Nocturne,* and cross over to the neighborhood café. Workers are jackhammering the street, the deafening vibrations pervade the walls of the café. Unable to write, I read, traipsing the *Nocturne* network—uncertain streets, fragments of addresses, routes no longer relevant, and events that add up to a circle of nothing. I lament not writing but figure losing oneself in the energized torpor of the Modiano universe is almost like writing. You enter the skin of the narrator with his pale sense of paranoia and preoccupation with minutiae and the space around you shifts. Inevitably somewhere midsentence, I find myself reaching for my pen.

Reaching the end of *Nocturne,* though not really an end, as vapors of future seep beyond the last page, I reread the beginning, then fast-forward to my own day ahead. I am set to leave on the last flight to Paris. My French publisher has arranged a week of book-related events that include speaking to journalists about writing. My notebook remains untouched. A writer who isn't writing going to talk with journalists about writing. What a know-it-all, I chide myself. I have another black coffee and a bowl of blueberries. There is plenty of time and I am a light packer.

The street a construction zone, I am obliged to wait before crossing back home while a massive crane hoists metal support beams several floors above the café, bringing to mind the opening scene in *La Dolce Vita* where a helicopter transports a life-size figure of Christ above the urban rooftops of Rome.

I gather my usual things for travel, setting them in a pile next to my small suitcase as I listen again to the voice-over of the trailer. The lilt of an unfamiliar language implies the saddest of melodies suffusing. As troops advance, a young mother hangs clothes and shields her eyes from the sun. Her husband is separating the wheat from the chaff, her daughter happily at play. Intrigued, I search a bit more and find a six-minute cut from *Risttuules* subtitled *The Birch Letter*. A shot of an open window, images of whiteness and birch trees emerging through whispered phrases and a train and the wind and the void.

The phone rings, breaking the spell, my flight canceled. I have to make an earlier one. I swiftly get in gear, call a taxi, slide my computer in its case, camera in a sack, and cram the rest into the suitcase. The taxi arrives too quickly as I realize I haven't yet chosen what books to take. The prospect of boarding a plane without a book produces a wave of panic. The right book can serve as a docent of sorts, setting a tone or even altering the course of a journey. I desperately scan the room as if searching for a lifeline in a deep marsh. Among a small pile of unread books atop my flat files are Francine du Plessix Gray's monograph on Simone Weil and Modiano's *Pedigree*, with the astonished face of the author on the cover. I snatch them up, say goodbye to my little Abyssinian cat, and head to the airport.

Luckily traffic is thin as we enter the Holland Tunnel. Relieved, I sink back into the voice of Erma. I imagine writing a story guided by the atmosphere conjured by the resonance of a particular human voice. Her voice. No plot in mind, just trailing her tones, timbres, and composing phrases, as if music, and superimposing them, transparent layers, over hers.

And the face of love is nothing but the whiteness of winter blanketing limbs of trees fallen through holes colorless skies.

I hurry through the terminal, easily making my flight yet somewhat thrown off. There is no hope of falling asleep this early, to say nothing of the fact that my hotel room won't be ready for several hours after I arrive. Nonetheless I settle in, drink mineral water, and let myself be drawn into the book of a life, a shard of Simone Weil. The hastily chosen book was to prove itself more than serviceable and the subject an admirable model for a multitude of mindsets. Brilliant and privileged, she coursed through the great halls of higher learning, forfeiting all to embark on a difficult path of revolution, revelation, public service, and sacrifice. I had not as yet dedicated time or study to her, but that would surely change. Closing my eyes, I envision the tip of a glacier and slide into an intimate hot spring surrounded by walls of impenetrable ice.

ÉGLISE DE SAINT-GERMAIN-DES-PRÉS

2

I pass through customs and sleepily exit the terminal at Paris-Orly. My friend Alain awaits me. I check into my hotel located on a narrow street just steps away from the church in Saint-Germain-des-Prés. As they prepare my room, we have baguettes and coffee at Café de Flore.

Saying goodbye, I enter the small park adjacent to the church with Picasso's bust of Apollinaire at the entrance. I sit on the same bench where I had sat with my sister in the spring of 1969. We were in our early twenties, when everything, including the sentimental head of the poet, was a revelation. Inquisitive sisters with a handful of precious addresses of cafés and hotels. The Deux Magots of the existentialists. The Hôtel des Etrangers, where Rimbaud and Verlaine presided over the Circle Zutique. The Hôtel de Lauzun with its chimeras and gilded halls where Baudelaire smoked hashish and penned the opening poems in *Les fleurs du mal*. The interior of our imaginations glowed, as we walked back and forth before these places synonymous with poets. Just to be near where they had written, sparred, and slept.

It is suddenly chilly. I notice bits of bread, relentless pigeons, a young couple's languorous kisses, and a homeless fellow with a long beard in an overcoat seeking a few coins. Our eyes meet and I get up and walk toward him. His eyes are grey and he reminds me of my father. A silvery light seems to spread over Paris. I feel a wave of nostalgia induced by the perfect present. It begins to drizzle. Grainy bits of film swirl. The Paris of Jean Seberg in a striped boatneck shirt hawking the *Herald Tribune*. The Paris of Eric Rohmer, standing in the rain in the Rue de la Huchette.

Later in the hotel, struggling to stay awake, I open the Weil biography at random, nod off briefly, then pick up in an entirely new section, the process somehow animating the subject. Simone Weil walking brusquely into the frame from the third dimension. I see the edge of her long cloak and her thick dark hair brutally cropped like that of the brilliant, independent bride of Frankenstein.

Yet another image of Simone flits past my eye, a caricature like those of the voyagers to *Mount Analogue* sketched by René Daumal. Heart-shaped face, hair horizontally jutting, dark probing eyes behind round wire-rim glasses. They knew each other and he had taught her Sanskrit. I picture the consumptive pair, their heads barely touching, poring over ancient texts, their failing systems thirsting for milk.

The hand of gravity is pulling me under. Switching on the TV, I flip through channels, stopping at the tail end of a documentary on the staging of Racine's *Phaedra,* then fall into a heavy asleep. A few hours later I suddenly open my eyes. On the screen a girl on ice. Some kind of figure skating championship. A sturdy blonde finishes her program successfully. The girl following her is charming but has a bad fall and cannot regroup. I remember watching such competitions with my father, sitting at his feet while he brushed my tangled hair. He admired the athletic skaters, I the graceful ones who seemed to incorporate classical ballet.

The last skater is announced, a sixteen-year-old Russian, the youngest in competition. Despite being half awake I give her my full attention. A young girl steps onto the ice as if nothing else exists. Her single-minded purpose, combination of innocent arrogance, awkward grace, and daring is breathtaking. Her triumph over the others brings me to tears.

In my sleep genius combines, regenerates. Simone's determined heart-shaped face merges with the face of the young Russian figure skater. Dark cropped hair, dark eyes penetrating darker skies. I climb the side of a volcano carved from ice, heat drawn from the well of devotion that is the female heart.

~

I wake early, walk over to Café de Flore and have a plate of ham and eggs and black coffee. The eggs are perfectly round, set upon a perfectly round slab of ham. I marvel how genius manifests, in a plate of eggs or the center of a rink. Alain joins me and we head over to 5, Rue Gaston-Gallimard, the publishers' headquarters since 1929. My editor Aurélien opens the door to Albert Camus's former office. From the sole window a view of the garden below. Displayed in a case are books of Simone Weil's, posthumously published under his direction. *Lettre à un religieux, La connaissance surnaturelle,* and *L'enracinement.*

Mr. Gallimard greets me in his office. On the mantle is the clock that Saint-Exupéry had presented to his grandfather. We descend worn marble stairs, pass through the blue salon, and enter the garden where Yukio Mishima was photographed sitting in a white rattan chair. We stand for several moments silently admiring the garden's geometric simplicity.

It brings to mind other gardens, like stereo cards streaked with time. The centuries-old Orto Botanico in Pisa with its forgotten statue of Humboldt and towering Chilean wine palms. The Garden of Simples, with its wild medicines, where consciousness alternately expands and finds peace. I think of Joseph Knecht, alone in the unassuming garden of scholars, contemplating his future as Magister Ludi. The garden at Schiller's summer home in Jena, where Goethe was said to have planted a gingko tree.

—I knew Genet, Mr. Gallimard says softly, looking away so as not to appear immodest.

I am lured by a number of spirals carved on the high wall to the right. They resemble the spiral Brancusi created to represent James Joyce for the small Black Sun edition of *Tales Told by Shem and Shawn.* I linger, content to be with the ghosts of writers who have passed into this same perimeter. Camus leaning against the wall smoking cigarettes. Nabokov reflecting on the curve of the Nautilus.

GALLIMARD GARDEN

That night I dreamt I knew how to swim. The sea was cold, but I had a coat on. I awoke shivering, having left the window open to look at the church before I turned in. I could see the church from my window and thus a long stretch of my life. I had first seen this church with my sister in late spring of 1969. We entered it together somewhat timidly and lit candles for our family.

I get up to close the window. It is raining, silent steady rain. I suddenly begin to cry.

—Why are you crying? Asks a voice.

—I don't know, I answer. Maybe because I'm happy.

~

Paris is a city one can read without a map. Walking down the narrow Rue du Dragon, old Sépulcre Street, which once boasted an imposing stone dragon. No. 30 a plaque in memory of Victor Hugo. Rue de l'Abbaye. Rue Christine. No. 7, Rue des Grands Augustins, where Picasso painted *Guernica*. These streets are a poem waiting to be hatched—suddenly it's Easter; eggs everywhere.

I walk aimlessly, finding myself in the Latin Quarter, then cut over to Boulevard Saint-Michel, searching for number 37, where Simone was raised and the Weil family lived for decades. I have a flash of Patrick Modiano tracing one address after another, crisscrossing the entire city in search of a certain stairway. I think of Albert Camus, about to receive the Nobel

Prize, making this same pilgrimage to the Weil residence, but for graver reasons – not mere curiosity but contemplation.

A burgeoning routine. Awake at seven. Café de Flore at eight. Read until ten. Walk to Gallimard. Journalists. Book signing. Lunch with the Gallimard crew – Aurélien, Cristelle, duck confit and beans, local café fare. Tea in the blue salon, the garden beyond, interviews. A journalist hands me a book on Simone Weil, translated into English. Do you know of her, she asks. Later a journalist named Bruno presents me with an image of Gérard de Nerval, which I place on my night table. It is the same melancholy portrait I had taped above my desk when in my twenties.

Alain and I meet in the evening and have a light meal as he briefs me on our journey in the morning to southern France. A book presentation is scheduled in Sète, an old seaside resort on the Mediterranean, the native town of the poet Paul Valéry. Happy with the prospect of visiting a new place and breathing the salt air, I return to my room, pack light, and then attempt to cajole myself to sleep, reciting my mantra: *Simone and Patrick. Patrick and Simone.* He imbues anxious calm. She fills me with adrenaline, dangerously familiar.

I wake earlier than usual, arrive at the Flore just as it opens, order a baguette with fig jam and a black coffee. The bread is still warm. On the way to the train I recheck the contents of my sack. Notebook, Simone, underwear, socks, toothbrush, a folded shirt, camera, my pen and dark glasses. Everything I need. I have hopes of writing but instead stare

CUTLERY. CAFÉ DE FLORE

sleepily out the train window, noting the changing landscape as we pass from the graffiti-scrawled walls in the outskirts of Paris to more open spaces, sandier ground, scruffy pine, and finally the pull of the sea.

In Sète we have fresh seafood at a local café overlooking the harbor. Alain and I walk up a hill to the cemetery in search of Paul Valéry. We find him and pay respects, but the grave of a young girl named Fanny who loved horses also beckons. Friends and family have placed horses on her headstone, forming a little stable undisturbed by weather or vandal. Drawn to yet an older headstone, I note the word *DEVOUEMENT* carved diagonally on the border. I ask Alain what it means.

—Devotion, he answers, smiling.

The following morning before rejoining Alain and Aurélien at the train station, I take a last walk, discovering a sequestered park presided over by an imposing statue of Neptune. I climb uneven stone steps up a slope that opens onto what appears to be a botanical garden, with a number of squat palms, and a variety of trees. As I wander about, an unexpected though familiar giddiness overcomes me, an intensification of the abstract, a refracting of the mental air.

The sky a pale green, the atmosphere releases a relentless flow of images. I take refuge on a bench protected by shadows. Slowing my breath, I unearth my pen and notebook from my sack, and begin scribbling, somewhat involuntarily.

A white dragonfly plucked from a music box. A Fabergé egg encasing a miniature guillotine. A pair of skates twisting in space. I write of trees, a repetition of figure-eights, the magnetic pull of love. Not certain of how much time has passed, I cease writing, rush past the curving back of Neptune, down the stone steps, hurrying to the nearby train station. Alain regards me quizzically. Aurélien asks me whether I took any photographs. Only one, I say, a picture of a word.

On the train I continue to write feverishly, as though resuscitated from a sea of memory. Alain glances from his book and looks out the window. Time contracts. We are suddenly approaching Paris. Aurélien is sleeping. It occurs to me that the young look beautiful as they sleep and the old, such as myself, look dead.

3

A particular joy of good weather, an amiable lightness I easily succumb to. I go into the Saint-Germain church where boys are singing. Communion perhaps. There is a solemn delight in the air and I feel a familiar desire to receive the body of Christ but do not join them. Instead I light a candle for my loved ones and the parents who lost children at Bataclan. The candles flicker before Saint Anthony holding a babe, both covered with decades of delicate graffiti that make them seem alive, animated by the inscribed pleas of the living.

I take a last walk up the Rue de Seine, or is it down? I don't know, I just walk. There is the odd familiarity that

VOLTAIRE. SQUARE HONORÉ-CHAMPION

keeps tugging at me. A long-ago sense of things. Yes. I have been on this same path with my sister. I stop and look at the narrow lane of Rue Visconti. I had so thrilled at my first sight of it that I ran the length and jumped in the air. My sister took a picture and in it I see myself, forever frozen in air full of joy. It seems a small miracle to reconnect with all that adrenaline, all that will.

At the top of Square Honoré-Champion, another flash of recognition. Toward the back of a rather pedestrian garden I recognize a statue of Voltaire, the first thing I photographed in Paris. Amazingly the little garden remains as pristine and uninteresting as it was half a century ago, but Voltaire, much changed, seems to be laughing at me. The details of his once benevolent face, worn away by time, appear darkly comic, macabre, as slowly decomposing he stoically presides over his unchanging domain.

I remember seeing Voltaire's cap in a glass case in a museum somewhere. A very humble flesh-colored lace cap. I harbored an intense desire for it, a strange fascination that lingered coupled with a superstitious notion that the wearer might access the residue of Voltaire's dreams. All in French of course, all of his period, and at that moment it occurred to me that dreamers through time dreamed of those in their own epoch. The ancient Greeks dreamed of their gods. Emily Brontë of the moors. And Christ? Perhaps he did not dream, yet knew all there was to dream, every combination, until the end of time.

~

My duties to Gallimard accomplished, I board the Eurostar to London. On the train I rewrite some of the passages of the story I had begun in the quiet park in Sète and continued on the racing train to Paris. Initially I wondered what prompted me to write such an obscure, unhappy tale. I did not wish to dissect with a surgeon pen, but as I reread I was struck by how many passing reflections and occurrences had inspired or permeated it. Even the most insignificant reference I saw clearly as if highlighted. For instance, a perfect plate of fried eggs was echoed in a round pond. I had drawn certain aspects of Simone's countenance for Eugenia, my young heroine: her intellectual flexibility, strange gait, and innocent arrogance. Yet other aspects I reversed. Simone shuddered at the touch of another, while Eugenia blatantly craved it.

At St. Pancras International I took yet another train to Ashford, the last length of my journey, to find Simone Weil's grave. We passed row houses, a lifeless landscape. I noticed the date on my ticket was June 15, the birthday of my late brother Todd. His only child a daughter called Simone. I immediately brightened. Only good could happen today.

Arriving, I found a coffee stand, then looked for a taxi. The sky was deepening and there was a strong chill in the air. I removed my camera and watch cap from my suitcase. The taxi ride took about fifteen minutes and I was dropped off in front of the entrance of the Bybrook Cemetery. I half expected there would be a little stone carriage house or someone distributing maps, but there was no one. Only a groundskeeper cutting weeds in a veil of light but steady rain.

The cemetery was more sprawling than I anticipated and I had no idea where Simone might be. I walked up and down paths, somewhat daunted. The light was low. Only noon, yet more like sundown. I took a few photographs. An embedded cross. An ivy-encrusted tomb. Nearly an hour passed. It continued to rain. A part of me was succumbing to the notion that it was an impossible task when I suddenly remembered she was buried in the Catholic sector. I found an area with many likenesses of Mary and crosses everywhere, but no trace of Simone. I searched an area dense with statues. The sky grew darker. I sat on a bench somewhat demoralized. Would Simone approve of this pilgrimage? I thought not. But I had lavender from Sète in an old handkerchief to leave her, small bits of France, and recalling her love of her homeland, her longing to return, I pressed on.

I looked up at the menacing clouds.

I entreated my brother.

—Todd, can you help me? I'm alone on your birthday and searching for someone named Simone.

I felt his hand guiding me. On my right was a wooded area and I felt compelled to walk toward it. Suddenly I stopped. I could smell the earth. There were larks and sparrows, a small shaft of light that appeared, then disappeared. I turned my head with no exalted pause and found her, in all her modest grace. I opened the bellows of my camera, adjusted my lens and took a few pictures. As I knelt to place the small bundle beneath her name, words formed, tumbling like a nursery song. I felt helplessly at peace. The rain dissipated. My shoes were muddied. There was an absence of light, but not of love.

4

Fate has a hand but is not the hand. I was looking for something and found something else, the trailer of a film. Moved by a sonorous though alien voice, words poured. I went on a journey lured by a jukebox of lights conjuring a symphony of reference points. I threaded a world that was not even my own, wandering the abstract streets of Patrick Modiano. I read a book, introduced to the mystic activism of Simone Weil. I watched a figure skater, wholly beguiled.

I began to write the piece entitled *Devotion* on the train from Paris to Sète. Initially I thought to compose a heightened discourse between disparate voices – a sophisticated, rational man and a precocious, intuitive young girl. I was interested to see where they would lead each other, forming an alliance in a realm of opulence and obscurity. I had also kept a loosely formed travel diary: bits of poems, notes, and observations for no particular reason save to write. Looking back on these fragments, I am struck with the thought that if *Devotion* was a crime, I had inadvertently produced evidence, annotating as I went along.

Most often the alchemy that produces a poem or a work of fiction is hidden within the work itself, if not embedded in the coiling ridges of the mind. But in this case I could track a plethora of enticements, a forest of firs, Simone Weil's haircut, white bootlaces, a pouch of screws, Camus's existential gun.

I can examine how, but not why, I wrote what I did, or why I had so perversely deviated from my original path. Can one, tracking and successfully collaring a criminal, truly comprehend the criminal mind? Can we truly separate the how and the why? A few moments of self-interrogation forced me to acknowledge the strange remorse I felt following the writing of it. I wondered, since I had birthed my characters, if I was mourning them. I also considered whether it was a quality of age, for when young I wrote with reckless abandon on any subject without a shred of moral concern. I let *Devotion* stand as written. You wrote it, I told myself, you can't wash your hands of it like Pilate. I reasoned these concerns philosophical, or even psychological. Perhaps *Devotion* is merely itself, unfettered by worldview. Or perhaps a metaphor drawn from the untraceable air. That is my final conclusion, one that is absolutely meaningless.

Back in New York City, I found it difficult to chemically readjust. More than that, I suffered bouts of nostalgia, a yearning to be where I had been. Having morning coffee at Café de Flore, afternoons in the Gallimard garden, bursts of productivity on a moving train. I was on Paris time, dropping off to sleep in the late afternoon, waking suddenly in the long, still night. On one such night I watched *The Secret Garden*. A crippled boy made to walk again through the fervent will of a lively young girl. There was a time when I imagined I would write such stories. Like *Sara Crewe* or *The Little Lame Prince*. Orphaned children negotiating a darkness eclipsed in brightness. Not the type of story I found myself writing breathlessly on a Paris train without remorse.

Silence. Passing cars. The rumble of the subway. Birds calling for dawn. I want to go home, I whimpered. But I already was.

BYBROOK CEMETERY, ASHFORD, KENT

Ashford

Deep in the earth your little bones
your little hands your little feet
in restless repose unfastening loops
calling for bread and potato soup
a shock of light struck the valve
milk of the lamb poured from the side
and a terrible mist rose underfoot
you were all snow white
and I the seventh dwarf
prepared to serve you
there were wafers enough
for every living thing
who offered his tongue
there were no more cries
there was no fasting heart
Only the relics of consumption
wrapped in the silk of existence

Devotion

1

He first noticed her on the street. She was small with porcelain skin and thick dark hair with severely cut fringe. Her cloak seemed thin for winter and the hem of her uniform uneven. As she brushed past he felt the sting of intellect. A petite Simone Weil, he remembered thinking.

He saw her again a few days later, heading away from the other students, rushing to make their class. He stopped and turned, speculating on what drove her in the opposite direction. Perhaps she felt ill and broke form to return home, but her determined air suggested otherwise. Most likely a forbidden rendezvous, an eager young man. She boarded a trolley. He didn't know why he followed her.

Absorbed in her own trajectory, she failed to notice him when she reached her destination. He stayed several paces behind as she approached the bordering forest. Unwittingly she led him down a stony path to a thick grove obscuring a large pond, perfectly round, and completely frozen. Between incisions of light cutting through the dense pine, he observed as she brushed the snow from a low, flat boulder then sat gazing toward the glistening pond. Clouds moved overhead, masking then exposing the sun, and momentarily the scene surreally solarized. She suddenly turned in his direction, but did not see him. She removed a pair of battered ice skates from her satchel, stuffed crushed paper in the toes and dutifully wiped their blades.

The surface of the pond was patchy, her skates ill fitting. Adjusting to these hindrances may have contributed to her perilous style. After circling several times, she picked up speed and from a seemingly teetering position effortlessly cast herself into the liquid space. Her jumps had astonishing elevation; her landings were offset, yet precise. He watched as she executed a combination spin, bending and twirling like a mad top. Never had he seen athleticism and artistry so poignantly meshed.

There was a wet chill in the air. The sky deepened, casting a blue light on the pond. She opened her eyes wide, catching the blur of pines in the distance, the bruised sky. She skated for those trees, that sky. He should have turned away, but knew himself, recognizing the interior shudder when face to face with a delicacy: as a vessel, wrapped in centuries of rags, that he would unwind, surely possess, and raise to his lips. He left before the snow fell, catching sight of her raised arm as she spun, head bowed.

The wind picked up, and reluctantly she left the pond. Untying her laces she reflected with satisfaction on the day's events. She had risen early, said prayers in the student chapel, and having already completed her national exams, retrieved her satchel from her locker and left without hesitation or remorse. Though a star pupil, precocious in her studies, she was completely indifferent. She had mastered Latin at twelve, easily solved complex equations, and was more than capable of breaking down and reexamining the most ambiguous concepts. Her mind was a muscle of discontent. She had no intention of completing her studies, not now or ever; she was almost sixteen, finished with all that. Her sole desire was to astonish, all else faded as she stepped upon the ice, feeling its surface through the blades into her calves.

A misted morning that would soon clear, making it perfect for skating. She made coffee and warmed some bread in a pan and called out to her Aunt Irina, forgetting that she was now on her own. On the way to the pond she noticed that despite the cold there were berries in the brambles, but she did not pick them. Wisps of fog seemed to rise from the ground. The light was silvery, and the pond took on a burnished quality, as if finished by munificent hands. She made the sign of the cross and stepped upon the ice, reveling in her solitude. But she was not alone.

An intemperate curiosity and the certainty that he would find her drove him to return. Undetected, he watched as she executed unique and intricate combinations, danger-ously and poetically sporadic. Her rapture excited him; God had given breath to a work of art. She arched her body, spin-ning in descending and ascending spirals, shaking a bit of glittering dust from the star she was undeniably becoming. He soon departed but not soon enough.

She could not be sure of the exact moment she became conscious of his presence. At first it was no more than a feel-ing, then slyly one morning she distinguished his form, the colors of his coat and scarf, not entirely camouflaged. Sensing no ill will, she continued to skate, energized by his presence. No one, not even her aunt, had seen her skate, since she was eleven. As the days passed guardedly connected, they assumed their roles, each bolstered by the other.

Having freed herself from the enforced structure of school, and Irina gone, her days flowed into one another. She had little sense of time and lived by the approach and dimin-ishing of light. She slept longer than usual and dawn was already breaking. Hurriedly she moved through morning rit-uals, grabbed her skates and headed toward the grove. As she approached the pond she spied the edge of a large white box set by the exposed roots of an old sycamore. She knew it must be for her, from Him. Dropping her skates, she removed a few heavy stones that had been placed on the lid and opened it slowly. Within layers of pale tissue was a mauve colored coat, a costly though somewhat old-fashioned garment,

ingeniously cut and lined with silky fur. It suited her perfectly, as the princess-style skirt was detachable, so to practice freely. With trembling hands, she examined every detail,
marveling at the elaborate stitching, weightless fur lining,
and its strange color that seemed to change with the changing light.

She slipped it on, surprised that despite the impression
of lightness it provided the warmth of a miracle. She shyly
searched his usual site, to register her pleasure, but there was
no sign of him. Twirling about giddily, she experienced the
melancholy luxury of solitary joy.

The unexpected gift suggested small hopes, a vague but
promising human connection. She felt a delight but also a
fear of it, for it momentarily seemed to eclipse her impatience
to skate. She lived only for skating, she told herself; there
was no room for anything else. Not love, school, or scraping
the walls of memory. Negotiating a bouquet of confusion, the
lace on her skate broke in her hand. She quickly knotted it,
then unfastened the skirt of her new coat and stepped onto
the ice.

—I am Eugenia, she said, to no one in particular.

2

Cold rain streaked the windows of the cottage, then froze in strange patterns. There would be no skating this morning. Eugenia sat at the kitchen table and opened her journal. The first pages contained variations of the same set of lines, a poem of sorts, her loosely strung *Siberian Flowers*, written in the Estonian language of her mother and father, a language she had taught herself. She then turned to the back pages used primarily as an exercise book to practice English. Thoughts about skating, her aunt and former guardian Irina, and the parents she never knew. She intended to write more, but no words came to her, so she read and corrected what she had already written.

I was born in Estonia. My father was a professor. My parents had a nice house with some land and a beautiful garden that my mother tended with much devotion. My mother's younger sister Irina lived in our house. She was leaving the country with a gentleman named Martin Burkhart. He was twice Irina's age and very rich.

My father had a sense of impending danger. My mother had no such sense, she saw only good in people. My father entreated Martin to take me with them. Irina said my mother held me and cried for three days and nights. It comforted me to imagine being covered with my mother's tears. That spring my parents were separated and deported from their village in Estonia. My mother was sent to a Siberian work camp but nothing is known about what happened to my father. I have no memory of these things. I only know what Irina has told me. Not the names of my parents or our village, Martin believed it was too dangerous. Everyone was afraid then, even after the war was over, but I was only a child and feared nothing.

Irina was beautiful, like a film star, like Gene Tierney who I have seen in her movie magazines. Her overbite is the same, and the way she waved her hair. Martin took care of our papers, rations, and gave me his surname. He took care of everything. He was entranced by Irina's beauty as someone with an object in a museum behind a wall of glass. She could be somewhat haughty but that seemed to amuse him and he bought her many presents.

Martin took great interest in me as I grew. He bought me a doll and pretty dresses. I had ballet lessons and a tutor who assured him I was excelling academically. On my fifth birthday he took us to an ice pageant. I remember this most of all.

After I saw the skaters I cried for three days and three nights. I cried as my mother cried. Perhaps I recognized my destiny but was too young to fully comprehend what that meant. Unable to resist tears, Martin soon bought me skates, and a white muff for my hands with a matching hat. When I first stepped onto the ice I faltered, not out of fear, but excitement, for something wonderful happened. Everything I needed was revealed to me in a split second, like suddenly knowing all the answers to a difficult test, or the exact route to an impossible destination.

I saw it all before me, in an instant that instantly disappeared, yet made its mark. I intuited that when I was ready I held the key. I did so well that soon skating lessons were added to ballet, and not too long after, ballet slowly abandoned. I had what I needed from it. I would simply synthesize ballet and skating. After that it was the same with everything. Martin taught me to play chess. I was a worthy opponent but I didn't care about winning. I was mostly interested in the moves and how I could incorporate them in a routine. I never spoke of this, for I was afraid he might insist I spend less time thinking of skating. Martin said I was gifted in science, but this gift gave me no tools to express the inexpressible. We spoke many languages together, even dead ones. Yet of all the languages I have known, skating is the one I know best. A language without words, where the mind must bow to instinct.

And then everything changed. Martin died suddenly from a stroke of the heart. We weren't allowed to go to the funeral. His solicitor sent Irina a check and the keys to the house on a small piece of land bordering the forest. We had to leave the apartment he had provided for us. With the money he left her, we lived comfortably, but nothing was ever as good as that time. Only when I found the secret pond did I understand why he had chosen this house. I was almost eleven. He must have known I would find it. But there was nothing there that made Irina happy, not until she met Frank. Before that she moved through the days as if a ghost.

Irina has been gone for almost two months. I know she would be angry that I left school. But no one there will mind. My conflicting thoughts and questions have always made my teachers uncomfortable and I believe there is nothing more they can teach me. I understand why Irina left; there has never been much affection between us. I have been a responsibility that she was obliged to accept. Yet I have some misgivings about my behavior when she said goodbye. My heart was quite hard. I said nothing. Perhaps because I was afraid, for she is my only link with my family.

Eugenia stopped reading for a moment and then added the words — *She is my family.* Laying down her pencil, she realized she truly regretted not helping Irina make their parting easier. Perhaps receiving the gift from the stranger somehow disarmed her, his unbidden generosity exposing her young heart unduly hardened. She glanced toward the window and noticed the rain had turned to a light snow. Closing her journal, she slipped on the coat, threw her skates over her shoulder and walked through the forest to the pond. She skated until the sun retreated. Afterward she sat on the flat boulder, taking her time to unlace the boots of her skates and examine the blades. She had no fear of returning home in the dark; she had trod the same path a thousand times and knew every stone underfoot.

The moon rose, illuminating the pond. It was more miniature lake than pond, and surprisingly deep, her secret salvation from the oppressive atmosphere of the lonely little cottage, which had always seemed a prison to Irina. Until she met Frank, as handsome as she was beautiful, the one who finally made her happy, the one who took her away.

The day Irina left she wore no makeup and was crying. It occurred to Eugenia how young she looked, and how she seemed like an actress playing out a scene rehearsed many times.

—I have to leave. Frank is waiting for me. He gave me some money for you, it is on the dresser. Soon you will be sixteen. You will do fine, just as I did.

Eugenia stood in silence. She wanted to reach out to her, thank her for all of her sacrifices, but she could not find the right words. Only a swirl of questions that would remain forever unanswered.

—Don't hate me, I did my best. I am already thirty-two; this is my chance to have something for myself.

As she reached to open the door she stopped and looked at Eugenia in desperation.

—I was born beautiful, she blurted, why should I have an ugly life?

And then she was gone. Like mother and father, like Martin, like the washing on the line.

The stars appeared as if shaken from a net. Eugenia sat beneath them, continuing to reflect. Each star plays its part; each has its own place. Everything I am, she was thinking, has been given to me by nature.

3

He was a solitary man, in his late thirties, of unusual control, hardy and virile, yet uniquely sensitive, having already negotiated the spectrum of academics, risk, art, and excess. A dealer in artifacts, rare manuscripts, and arms, he could easily identify the age and origin of an obscure ivory by feel, by the way it absorbed or reflected light. The valuable he delivered to museums; the exquisite he kept for himself. He had traveled extensively though not in leisurely fashion. His trunks contained a wealth of objects that when sold would add considerably to his fortune. He had done well, but the thrill of attainment had become hollow; he found himself uncharacteristically restless and short-tempered.

She had skated through his waking hours. He pictured her egocentrically spinning in her palace of ice. He imagined glimpsing her moving through crowds in faraway places, her thick dark hair, no hat or scarf, a battered pair of ice skates thrown over her small shoulder. The little witch, he was thinking, yet chided himself for attributing such power to an awkward schoolgirl.

In a dream he sat at a table observing the vast grounds of an unfamiliar colonial estate. The ghost of her, fragile as a steeple of spun sugar, materialized in the bright green field. She turned slowly in a wispy red dress, accentuating her lanky frame. He watched her with pleasure as she accelerated spinning, her double-jointed arms bending easily in the light wind.

— She will never be truly yours, whispered the woman serving him. He looked at her hard.

— Did you speak? he asked somewhat irritably.

— No, monsieur, she said, without a trace of emotion.

He awoke feeling inexplicably hemmed in, a vague sense of rage. He threw on a robe and sat in the drawing room, lighting a cigar and losing himself in the blue whorls of smoke.

≈

Several days passed and he did not come. In truth she missed his presence, which seemed to have inexplicably inspired her. Once again she was skating solely for herself. It was still very cold, but with her coat, and a happy absence of wind, she was able to skate for great lengths of time. The pond was her home, the act of skating her lover. She gave herself completely, generating her own heat.

Each year she dreaded the coming of spring, for soon the ice would vein underfoot and the surface of the pond would crack: like a hand mirror dropped on a marble floor. Just a little longer, she implored nature, just a week, a few days, a few more hours. She knelt on the ice. Not yet dangerous, but soon.

She did not see him, but felt him, sensed he was drawing nearer, and then suddenly she saw his coat. He remained in view but maintained his distance, satisfied with their silent commune. She didn't acknowledge his return yet accepted him without reproach. Crossing her arms over her heart she propelled herself, reaching a higher elevation than ever before. Emboldened by his presence, she entered her third turn, extending an arm above her, fingertips brushing the breadth heaven. She cried out involuntarily. *Would that I could die this moment.* Just a folly, a teenage prayer, a moment exquisitely mastered.

He withdrew, pierced.

At dawn she had cold coffee, a bowl of berries, and some bread she had made the night before. The sun was already high, troubling her, as she was hoping winter would last a while longer. As she reached the pond, she saw that he was already there, waiting. She set down her skates and approached him without trepidation, accessing a natural arrogance. He greeted her cordially in Swiss-German, but detecting his accent, Eugenia answered him in Russian. He was taken aback, yet pleased.

—Are you Russian? he asked.

—I was born in Estonia.

—You are a long way away.

—I was brought here as an infant by my aunt during the war. The pond is my home.

— How many languages do you speak?

— Several, she answered smugly. More than the fingers of your hands.

— Your Russian is very good.

— Languages are like chess.

— And words are like moves?

They stood there in a silence that was not uncomfortable. She was thinking that they had only the experience of silence and the coat between them.

— The coat, she began. But he waved it away.

— The coat is nothing, little one. I can give you anything you could imagine.

— I don't care about such things. I only want to skate.

— The ice will soon fail you.

She lowered her eyes.

— I have a friend who is an important trainer from Vienna. You could skate all you want, through spring and summer until your pond is ready for you.

— What is the price of this privilege?

He stared at her openly.

— I only want to skate, she repeated.

He extended his card. She watched him depart in his dark overcoat; he was not a big man but the coat gave the impression of strength.

She waited until he disappeared down the path, then knelt down and pounded the ice with a rock. She could feel the vibration of water moving beneath the surface, layers of ice melting. She gazed unhappily at the sun as it filled the atmosphere with the warmth of its light. It was all so beautiful yet signaled the ushering of endless months without her greatest happiness. Her defining sense of self was completely entwined with the laces of her skates. Winter would melt into spring, into summer, and she would have no recourse but to wait for falling leaves to signal winters return. She felt for the card in her pocket. Stirred by a chorus of sensations, she was at once liberated and trapped.

4

It was the first day of spring. The light streamed into her window and spread across her coverlet. There were pictures of Eva Pawlik taped on the wall over her bed. Her skates were hanging from a hook beckoning, but the ice was already melting. She made herself some cocoa, then unfolded a small blanket she kept in a basket in the corner of her room. Irina had given it to her on the morning of her thirteenth birthday, having saved it through the years, waiting for the right moment. The blanket had been made for her by her mother, and pinned to it was a letter written by her father. At the time she could not read it, but she studied the language, translated it, and read it over and over. He wrote of lifting her in the air and delighting in the fact that she had his mother's eyes, deep brown eyes that seemed to contain everything. The blanket was like a soft peach and had tiny flowers stitched on the edges.

Thank you mother, she whispered, thank you father.

Eugenia mended Irina's old knit sweater, finding a long strand of her hair, and wondered if she would ever come back. Irina had raised her and harbored all there was to know of their history. It had always been difficult to draw anything out of her, though sometimes, when she had too much vodka, she would speak about the song of the wolves, the ice-covered trees, or the scent of the pink-and-white flowers that covered everything in spring. But nothing of her mother and father. Eugenia often searched for answers in the cold eyes of Irina.

— Don't look for your mother in me, she would say. You must find her in yourself.

— Do I look like her?

— I really couldn't say, she would answer impatiently, applying her lipstick.

— But have I her hair.

— Yes, yes.

— Do I have eyes like my father?

— Don't look back, Eugenia, she would counsel, slipping on her fox stole. Everything is before us.

Now I have a coat finer than hers, she thought ruefully.

But she would have given it gladly for just one new piece of the puzzle. She had nothing save a recurring dream, like a moving still from a grainy film — her mother shading her eyes from the sun and sheets unfurling on a line. Though separated too young for it to be a true memory, she clung to it as if it were. She stitched together any passing reference, simple recollection, new facet of an old story, entreating Irina to offer up some new small patch for the fragile quilt that added up to herself. She never asked for love, nor longed for affection, had no experience with boys, not even adolescent kisses. She only wished to know who she was, and to skate. That was all she desired.

Eugenia took the card from her coat pocket. He had offered her everything. Her own trainer, fine skates, a place to practice as much as she wanted. She laid the card on the table, tracing her finger over his name, *Aleksandr Rifa*, embossed in bold script, with an address written in hand beneath. His name was Alexander but to her he would always be Him.

That afternoon, he had opened the door and found her before him, small and defiant.

— Today is my birthday, she said. I am sixteen.

He welcomed her into a suite of rooms, displaying his worldly goods, precious icons, ivory crucifixes, heavy strands of pearls, trunks brimming with embroidered silks and rare manuscripts. He offered her anything she desired.

— I don't care about your fortune.

—Perhaps a token for your birthday.

—I only want to skate. That is why I am here.

He paused before a glass case housing an elaborately enameled egg. In spite of herself she was drawn to it, and he unlocked the case and set it before her.

—Open it, he said. It was a gift from a Czar to an Empress.

Inside was a tiny Imperial coach perfectly wrought in gold. He placed the coach in her hand, watching her reaction.

—Guess my name, she said.

—There are many names.

—But I have the name of a queen.

—There are many queens.

She followed him into the bedroom. She stood in silence as he slowly removed her clothes; but he could feel her pulse quicken. He took her slowly, surprisingly gentle, comforting her as she cried out in pain. He took her again in the night, arousing in her an unexpressed and startling appetite for pleasure.

In the morning he removed the sheet, spread with a blood-moth stain.

—This room will be yours, if you wish it. I will have someone buy you new sheets.

—No. I will buy my own sheets.

He made her breakfast as she washed. She approached him expectantly.

—I knew you were trouble when I saw you walking

toward me, he said, I felt you as you brushed against my coat.

—I did not see you then.

—Perhaps you felt me, as I felt you.

—No. I felt nothing.

Youth can be cruel, he mused, but he also knew how to make her suffer. He pressed against her and told her he had to go, whispering the name he has given her. Philadelphia.

—Why Philadelphia?

—Because, he breathed into her ear, it was once a hotbed for freedom.

She leaned against the wall.

—I want the contents of the little pouch you wear around your neck, she said suddenly as if in retaliation.

Startled, he hesitated, but could not refuse her.

—They are worthless souvenirs, just small screws and the firing pin of an old rifle.

—It must be important.

—It was the rifle of a poet.

—Where is it?

—It is somewhere safe, faraway. I removed the screws so no one could use it. Without them it's useless as a weapon. The pouch is stitched.

—Give it to me.

—That's what you want?

—Yes.

—Are you certain?

—Yes, she said unflinchingly.

—Then I must one day give you the rifle as well.

—As you wish.

—You're killing me, he said.

—You're killing me, she returned.

He left a large sum of money on a slip of paper. Go to this address and buy new sheets, this kind, and he wrote the name on the back and kissed her again. It took her a while to find the shop. There were long shelves with every kind of sheet imagined but she gravitated toward a glass case filled with robes and pajamas in flesh-colored silk. Instead of sheets, she chose a simple chemise from the case, using half the money, and then took a trolley to an entirely different sector. There was a small resale shop that sold bedding from various Chinese laundries. After a long search she found a slightly worn set of sheets with the name he had written on a tag. Italian sheets, slightly frayed, but they were much nicer than any sheets she had known.

After buying the sheets she stopped at a small restaurant and ordered her own steak, a big one, and a large mug of coffee. Every so often she would touch the little sack just below the hollow of her throat. It cost me a lot, she was thinking, not with regret, but with pride. *That is how I became Philadelphia,* she wrote later in her journal. *Like the city of freedom. Yet I was not free. Hunger is its own warden.*

5

He returned to her with small gifts. A pale rose sweater and a medal of St. Catherine, the patron saint of Estonia. But what she liked best was a magazine with pictures of ice skaters, with Sonja Henie on the cover. For a while she seemed strangely indolent and luxuriously compliant, allowing herself to be transported by the pollens of spring.

In their languid nights they glimpsed into one another's world. He spoke of a privileged life, his father a diplomat, his mother from a prominent Swiss family. Privately tutored, he excelled in languages, and was socially impeccable, yet internally restless, consumed by the desire to tear things apart and rearrange according to his own design. He found solace in the poet Rimbaud, who did so with words.

— Is he your poet? she asked, touching the little pouch.

Alexander gravitated toward the arts but acceded to his father's demands, studying engineering in Vienna. He was unhappy there, turned his back on his father, and joined the resistance in France. He came to understand that tearing things apart was a powerful aspect of human nature. He explored on his own and followed the poet's footsteps from the Gothard Pass to the Abyssinian plain.

He read her passages from *Une saison en Enfer*. She lay beside him, picturing the young Alexander leaving the university as she had left her academy. The hypnotic sound of his voice lured her to sleep. He continued to read, then placed the book aside to look at her, small and glowing with a trace of dampness below her navel, and was moved to rouse her from her slumber.

All of nature awakened, flourished. Eugenia told him her stories, as she had written in her exercise book, answering his questions in lilting monotone, an impassive voice-over from a phantom existence.

—Were you close to your father?

—I never knew either of my parents. They were deported from Estonia in the spring to a Siberian work camp.

—For what reason?

—No reason is required for the herding of people like sheep.

—A story full of holes.

—Some things melt before they become memories. I remember trains. I remember new languages that I swiftly grasped. My aunt Irina sitting before a mirror, with her head tilted, brushing her hair.

—Tell me of Irina.

—She raised me, yet remains a mystery. She dreamed of going to America to be an actress, but the war changed everything. She had a beau who was more than twice her age, who was taking her away and my father begged him to take me as well. We crossed several borders and settled in Switzerland under his protection. He already had a family but he was as kind as he was rich. He bought me dresses and

Irina a gold charm bracelet.

— My mother's sister was beautiful; how else could she win a man so kind? He indulged her moods, and was moved by her uncomplicated delight with each new gift. I was five when he took us to an ice pageant. Never had I seen something so wonderful and yet I couldn't stop crying. I wanted to be her, the girl in the center of the ice. Even that young I knew that was my destiny. I could speak many languages by ear. I excelled in school yet nothing before skating gave me the tools to express the inexpressible. The world outside was rebuilding, but we lived in a bubble and I was too young to know of such things. After Martin died, Irina never brought anyone home, ever so often she would disappear, but she always returned. Not long after my fourteenth birthday she brought Frank home.

— Frank. Is he a good man?

— He is good for Irina, that I believe, as handsome as she is beautiful. Frank was an overseer in a construction company and has made a good living after the war. He made Irina laugh. He had to go away a lot for work, but when he was there things were better. Not long ago I grew out of my skates and took money from his pocket and bought a used pair, a bit too big, but good quality with fine blades. Irina asked me where I got the money and I told her. I thought Frank would be mad, but he wasn't. Let me see them, he said. I told him they were a bit big, but I stuffed the toes. Frank removed the blades and took them into town to have them sharpened.

That's the way he was. Irina was different with him than with Martin. She took off his shoes and rubbed his feet. Perhaps she was happy.

—Were you jealous of Irina?

—Jealous? Why should I be jealous? Irina cannot skate.

She got up for a moment and removed her slip.

He lay on the bed waiting. He gripped her hips. Slowly, Philadelphia, he said, and then rolled her on her stomach, gently prodding. When she cried out he turned her over. She felt his breath. She felt a pulse, like a small heart, and as she raised her hips she recalled the face of a boy who threw mud on her communion dress. She saw the smear and his dirty hands. She saw Irina's white lace glove. Outside the bells were tolling. She was swimming in filth, utterly lost.

6

Theirs was a story that could not resolve, only unravel. A story with the intrinsic power of myth. One that turned in on itself, leaving only a transparency, their bed an acrid cloud, on which they brutally coupled, then floated. When does it cease to be something beautiful, a faithful aspect of the heart, to become off-center, slightly off the axis, and then hurled into an obsessional void? He pondered this on an evening walk, stopping to flick his lit cigar into the fallen leaves. He watched them ignite, then smother in their own wetness.

When he went in on a business trip she could not help thinking of him. No, not really him, but what fanned between them, seeming to spread its warmth over the sacred pond, thawing its edges. She dreamed she was skating faster and faster, his voice whispering in her little shell ear. Philadelphia. She thrust herself above the ice, executing three revolutions, attempting a fourth. A magnificent leap was shattered by sun streaming in the window across her pillow as she opened her eyes.

Boarding the trolley she went back to the cottage to retrieve some of her things, She found two letters from the Academy waiting for her. Her National Scores were among the highest in the country, and she would receive a silver medal in mathematics. Little of this mattered to her. Despite a veil of light rain she took a walk through the woods. The path

6

6

leading to the pond was muddied. Before her, it appeared: a heavily misted diorama, strangely alien. It began to rain more heavily just as she took her place on the flat boulder, where she had sat since she was eleven. Abject, she bade her pond farewell and made her way back to the cottage. She slept in her old bed. The night turned cold and there was no wood for the fire. She awoke shivering, feverish.

In late morning she returned to his apartment, and lay on the bed in her room, small with one window, but it was hers. She remembered feeling this sick as a child. Martin told Irina to cut several white onions and boil them in a pot. Irina said the smell of onions would ruin her dress. He said he would buy her a new one. Eugenia had to bend over the pot and inhale the steam through her mouth. He stayed through the evening. Repeating the strangely solemn ritual. Peeling. Cutting. Boiling. Steaming. Breathing. She dreamed of her guardian, who had asked for nothing. He was always kind. There was always food and flowers. She had a bedroom with pale yellow walls and a doll with a dress that seemed to take on different colors in the morning light. Cream to pale rose to peach. She dreamed her mother dream. Sun, sheets on a line, and a woman, not unlike Irina, but with shorter, darker hair, shading her eyes from the sun.

Upon returning Alexander called out to her, but she failed to respond. He found her in her room lying awake in the dark. He approached her quizzically, but touching her throat, immediately grasped the situation. Eugenia was burning with fever. He filled the great claw tub with ice, and she lay in it shivering. After giving her something warm to drink, he carried her to his bed. She could feel his hands on her, his breath. She could feel herself slipping away.

Onions, she remembered whispering.

7

Alexander kept his promise. He asked to see her skates and removed the laces. You will no longer need them, he said, and gave her money for new skates, more than necessary. She was fitted with a flesh-colored pair with reinforced silk laces. They were perfect, made solely for her. Instead of crushed paper, her toes now feathered the tips of the boots. With the rest of the money she went to a small practice rink and slowly broke them in. It had been a long time since she had worn new skates. Her blisters were uncomfortable but a small price to pay. How miraculous it seemed to be able to skate when flowers were blooming.

Alexander introduced her to an Austrian coach named Maria. Eugenia sat quietly as the two of them discussed her as if she were a porcelain figurine without a tongue. Maria wrote down an address.

—Come tomorrow, she told her, and I will watch you skate. Earlier is best as the ice is resurfaced at night.

It was a large indoor arena with two rinks. Maria greeted her the following morning somewhat coldly.

—Your benefactor has given me a stipend for you to practice daily, for as long as you choose. I will observe you and give him my assessment.

Eugenia felt a bit manipulated but was elated by the prospect of unlimited time in the arena. Although Maria seemed unimpressed, she knew her own worth and felt confident as she laced up and entered her world. After a few times around the rink to feel out the space, any misgivings dissipated.

Maria was mystified by the young skater who seemed to appear from nowhere. Below average height, not conventionally pretty, yet striking with an odd sense of grace. There was something uniquely perceptive, even risky about her method; she skated on the brink. Though initially skeptical, the coach quickly recognized her charge's undeniable potential. Maria was to have her champion. Eugenia was to have her mentor, one who spoke her first language. The language of skating.

She came to call her coach Snezhana, for she was white as snow. Thick white sweaters to her knees, white leggings, and another white sweater wrapped around her waist. Her pale face, framed by unruly yellow hair, still retained some of its youthful beauty. Once she had captivated audiences with her ice-blue eyes and her steely performances. Emotion stripped of emotion. But a terrible accident had put an end to her escalating career. A sequence of operations had been successful, but she never recovered her remarkable dexterity, or her powerful athleticism.

A champion would provide her with some redemption for what she had lost. Maria, imposing her iron will, invested all she knew into Eugenia, attempting to refine, mold, give her the tools she needed to claim her destiny. But Eugenia could also be willful; she was ambitious but to what end? She dreamt not of laurels but of unprecedented action.

Alexander was preparing for a long journey. Eugenia confided their conflicts.

— Maria doesn't understand how I work. How I improvise the moves on my chessboard.

— Perhaps she suspects that you think too much.

— Every thought transforms as feeling. Skating for me is pure feeling, not the gateway to completion.

— She wants you to succeed.

— She wants me to perform within a traditional framework, to act out stories that seem unnatural.

— You have your own stories. You can convey them in your own style, your gestures. A mother's empty arms for example.

— My mother.

Eugenia fell silent and watched as he packed his trunk, emptying the contents of his dresser.

— Will you be gone long?

—For a long time, yes. But I will come back for you.

—Maria wants to take me to a skating camp in Vienna. She said I would need to get my papers in order.

—Maria seems quite possessive, he said.

Eugenia stiffened, yet she knew this was true; in a relatively short time Maria had inserted herself as mother and mentor.

She watched as his fingers moved across the delicate folds of the robe of an ivory Madonna. Her patina appeared more golden than white, from centuries of caresses.

—Are you taking her with you?

—Yes, she is my talisman for travel.

—You are also possessive, she said.

—Our possessions cause us much pain, he replied.

—How can that be when they give you such pleasure?

—Someone else will have them when I am dead. This causes me pain.

—I belong to no one, she said defiantly.

—No one? He smiled, unbuttoning her sweater.

Eugenia felt the unspoken pull between two forces. Both were controlling, but Alexander feigned indifference and thus drew her to him. During his absence Maria attempted to strengthen her influence. All her concentration was directed to ready Eugenia for competition. She had never seen such an innovative and daring skater, yet her unorthodox methods had to be tamed. In the process Eugenia felt oppressed, resisting discipline in favor of self-expression.

— We are preparing for a championship. There are rules. There is an entire system to embrace, then conquer.

—There are many ways to conquer.

Eugenia skated into the heart of the rink, and without hesitation performed a series of unfathomable combinations. In the silence of the arena she was entirely self-possessed, conjuring her own music. She was at that moment the legendary firebird rising from the ashes of a delicate nocturne, a blessing and a curse to her captors.

Maria was mesmerized by her young charge.

—Did you make a pact with the devil, some unholy deal? Maria laughed.

But Eugenia saw another truth within her eyes. Inside, Maria was not laughing.

Alexander returned without notice. Maria greeted him when he entered the arena; Eugenia did not see him, but felt him. He watched with satisfaction as she skated, catching the moment that she felt him near. Maria held her breath, astonished by the unprecedented height of her jump. His effect on the girl was not lost on her.

— She is doing very well, she told him, but needs further training. I want to take her to Vienna, where she will be exposed to a more competitive atmosphere. I understand her papers are not in order, she doesn't even have a proper passport. For a girl who knows so many languages it seems she has never been anywhere.

—I will see to it, he assured her, not wishing to betray his own plans for Eugenia's future. I will need to take her to Geneva for a few days while the embassy processes her papers. Then she will be free to travel as she wishes.

Eugenia continued to skate, oblivious to either of their designs. She had her own aspirations. An axel culminating in four rotations, why not five? The impossible reigned in the poem of her mind. To do what no other had done, to reinvent space, to produce tears.

8

She was sleeping in her own room. He woke her, and brought her coffee. We are leaving soon, take nothing, he said. I have everything we need.

—My papers? she asked sleepily.

—Yes, we have a 6 a.m. train to Geneva.

Using diplomatic connections, Alexander was able to obtain a passport for her. Yet they did not return as promised. Despite the strengths she had nurtured under Maria's aggressive tutelage, Eugenia allowed herself to be drawn away by him. In the beginning she was beguiled by their travels, the continuous motion of motorcars, trains, and ferries. She put out of her mind reoccurring images of Maria waiting, curiosity and desire eclipsing reason and responsibility.

She saw things that one sees only in books. The River Elbe. The bridge over the Danube. A spiraled steeple encasing a bomb. The Vieux-Marché where Jeanne d'Arc was burned, and the obscure room where the great map of the world was carved apart by victorious generals after the war. She walked barefoot on the stones that formed the uneven patio of the citadel of les baux. Alexander left an ivory cross in a niche quarried in the rock. They stood before it but they did not pray. She felt weary of travel but said nothing. In Marseille they laid flowers beneath the low window of a room at the Hospital of the Immaculate Conception before continuing a journey without repose.

— Where are we going?

— Far from here.

— Why must we go?

— To retrieve what I promised you.

— Can I skate? Is there a pond?

— No, Philadelphia, there are deep salt pools that will never freeze.

The sun was a burden. Everything seemed dead. How cruel you are, she was thinking. Yet she numbly followed him, like Trilby trailing her master.

They boarded a great ship. She tasted the salt in the air and shuddered. The sea was vast and the waves had beautiful curves. Eugenia imagined them frozen. She imagined the entire sea frozen so that she could spend her whole life skating on it and never reach the end. At the captain's table she stared intently at the centerpiece, a swan carved of ice, as it slowly melted. Lulled by the churning sea, she slept deeply, lifting one arm above her head, as she did when she skated. Looking down at her small naked body, Alexander felt a wave of remorse that he swiftly stifled.

Arriving at port they continued on, through miles of red dust, desert and savannah, until they reached a small compound surrounded by acacia and eucalyptus. A young man greeted Alexander in a dialect she did not know, and then welcomed her in French. His mother led them wordlessly to a room, which was annexed to theirs. It was spacious and washed with lime. The mat for sleeping was unrolled and there was a rifle against the wall. The woman brought them a thick broth, fermented bread, and cups of what smelled like the blood of an animal. The son killed a goat in their honor, and the woman burned chunks of frankincense.

Alexander rose before dawn, leaving her behind for several hours. He repeated this ritual daily, combing villages for sacred and discarded vestiges of their ancient culture, then returning to her in the evenings. The woman and her son tended to Eugenia as if she were a convalescing princess, serving her bowls of semolina and honey. They are trying to fatten me up, she was thinking, yet she ate greedily.

Unaccustomed to the heat, she slept more than usual. When she woke the woman would serve her a bitter-tasting drink with a sweet paste that did nothing to quench her thirst, but seemed to heighten her physical craving. Then she would wait, anticipating his return, their rapacious nights. Planets hung low in the black sky, dizzyingly close. All things seemed written on a shard of glass. She possessed not the glow of love but the face of a ravaged bird.

9

Stand here, Philadelphia, he said. He removed her scant garments and ran his fingers lightly over her body. His fingers were like feathers. He spoke of the first man, tracing the long Y of the Tigris and Euphrates. He switched languages seamlessly and she listlessly responded in kind. Suddenly he pressed her against the wall and she experienced in horror the potential bliss of unrequited desire.

In the evening the woman entered the room with bowls of sweet coffee. They sat on the dirt floor. The soiled sheets were a testament to their mutual ecstasy and sorrow. She removed the stained sheet and fitted the mat with a fresh one; the sight of it drew them to violate its brightness with mythic depravity. They were at once dogs and gods.

—Do you remember the first day you came to me?

—It was my birthday, she said, automatically clutching the pouch.

—Give it to me, he said. She sat up and reluctantly slipped it from her neck. It was very small on a leather string. He carefully unstitched the top; inside there were bits of ash and the minute screws and firing pin from the poet's rifle. He replaced the pin and the screws slowly, deliberately, and inserted a bullet then propped the rifle against the wall.

—Tomorrow, he said, I will teach you to shoot.

That night he tied her hands loosely with the laces of her old skates. He was gentle and kissed the lids of her closed eyes, moving down her naked throat. She threw her head to the side, opening her eyes. The laces barely made an impression, yet they dominated her dreaming, extending the length of a field, wriggling obscene things that covered ground, wrapped around the slim trunks of flowering trees, and entwined with the unruly yellow hair of Maria, her coach.

She awoke with terrifying clarity. The winding laces easily slipped from her wrists and she stealthily crawled away from the mat, reaching out for the rifle. She felt the same strain of nausea when moving through the woods with Frank, shooting her first rabbit, then watching him skin, stretch, and hang its small carcass to dry.

Eugenia rose. Alexander lay naked on the mat. It occurred to her he did not resemble such a god when he was sleeping. Her mind was spinning, inventorying all that he had given her, all that he had taken away. He opened his eyes and found her standing over him aiming low. He looked up sleepily, more amused than alarmed.

– Philadelphia, he said.

Raising the rifle slightly, she adjusted her aim.

– Philadelphia? He said searchingly, still struggling to wake.

– Yes, Philadelphia, a hotbed of freedom, she said, pulling the trigger.

There was a large sum in his valise. She kept her papers and handed half the money to the woman and gave his belongings, including his watch and cigars, to the son. At dawn they dug a hole and placed the body of Alexander Rifa into the earth with the rifle, his passport and the blood-spattered laces. They removed the screws and firing pin before burying him. Eugenia kept the screws and the medal he wore around his neck. It was silver and had a slice down the middle, as if glided over by the blade of a skate.

Before she departed, the old woman said something to her in Amharic. It was the first time she spoke directly to her, but Eugenia did not understand the dialect. The woman's son tried to explain what his mother had said. *A heart is stunned by another.*

The son helped her on the first difficult leg of her journey home. The travel was complicated and she moved slowly as if in a dream. Still possessing their tickets, she traveled by ship then a series of trains, sometimes just stopping in a city to roam unfamiliar streets. In Vienna she visited a museum and saw the golden cradle of a babe who became king. I have the name of a queen, she remembered saying. How long ago that seemed. It's a long way. It's a long way alone. There were bridges and lakes and botanical gardens. In Zurich she searched and found the grave of Martin Burkhart, who had treated her and Irina with such kindness, and laid flowers.

As she drew closer to home she vowed to never skate again. It was her penance, to deny herself the one thing she could not live without.

10

In the pocket of her skirt was the key to his apartment. She approached the heavy door carved with a crest of two lions embracing. She held her breath as she inserted the key, half expecting him to be there, waiting, perhaps with a small gift or a plan in mind for a luxurious punishment. The entrance room was dark, but the room he had given to her was flooded with light. Her little bed was still unmade from their hurried departure. The sight of it sickened her. There were a few dresses in the closet, and the pale rose sweater he had given her, still in its tissue.

She sat at the desk before a small stack of books he had chosen for her to read, determined to continue the education she had consciously shunned. A book on the *Golden Mean*, which had inspired a routine, built on an equation. And the large nautilus shell that he had presented her, noting how its exquisite curving spine echoed a spiraling turn on the ice. There was a photograph of a pond flanked by young pines and a cone that had retained the scent of the forest in its sticky resin. A kernel of remorse slowly opened and spread through her system; it was another kind of blood. She reached for the books yet unread, earmarked for studying English. *The Scarlet Letter* and *The Professor,* and the book he himself had been reading—the *Myth of Sisyphus,* with bits of commentary in Russian, in his elegant hand.

As if gently guided, she opened to the beginning and read, mentally translating his brief notations. The text posed a philosophic examination of the question of suicide—*Is life worth living?* He had written in the margin that perhaps there existed a deeper question—*Am I worthy of living?* Five words that shook her entire being. She rose abruptly, removed the photograph from its frame, slipped on the sweater, and left, careful to avoid the things that had been his.

11

The letter

Dear Eugenia,

So many times you asked me of our family, but I told you nothing. Your father gave me instructions to say nothing. Why should a child suffer the burden of politics, of blood? He truly feared for your safety. He was a professor and could speak several languages, just like you. His mother was Jewish; who died before you were born. Now I understand him. Your father was more political then religious. His outspoken ways caused him to be listed by the Soviets.

Our family was Catholic and your mother prayed all of the time. She cared mostly about her garden and you were her most precious flower. I feel nothing for my blood. I feel new, and Frank is new and our baby will be new. You are also new. That was the gift your parents gave you by releasing you.

Martin attempted to find our family. I hoped to return you to my sister and be free. But he found no one, nothing was like it was. I felt as if we were floating in space, and I felt frightened. But now I realize it was also a miracle. Having no past we have only present and future. We would all like to believe that we came from nowhere but ourselves, every gesture is our own. But then we find we belong to the history and fate of a long line of beings that also may have wished to be free.

There are no signs that tell us who we are. Not a star, not a cross, not a number on the wrist. We are ourselves. Your gift comes only from you. But Frank told me he once saw you skating on a small pond hidden in the woods. He was hunting a deer. He stopped and watched you but you did not see him. He told me you were a champion. That is exactly what he said.

Frank found us a nice house near the black forest. Sometimes I dream the wolves are crying. But all of that is over. I only want to be myself. I have a job selling perfume in a nice shop. I have several pretty dresses that I can wear again when the baby comes. We are safe and we are the new age.

Your Irina

12

At long last she returned to the cottage. A window was broken and the entrance was swept with dead leaves. There was a small pile of letters. The Academy, Maria, Irina. What would have happened had she continued her studies, stepped onto the rink of the world, if every move on the chessboard, every equation, even the dark fluidity of love had coalesced?

Winter struggled toward spring. Eugenia seldom left the cottage. She sat at the table before her journal and wrote in the shadows of heartache, slowly tracing the curves of letters as if by the blades of her skates. She added nothing to the brief essay of a life, only variations of the same poem, her *Siberian Flowers,* in a futile effort to uncover a father's eyes, a mother's face.

In her sleep she could hear the lyrical voice of Alexander. In her sleep she could hear her mother crying. Overflowing with the need to confess, to spill each indiscretion that led to the taking of another life, she boarded the trolley and went into the city, to the chapel attached to her former school.

—I yearn to pray, Father, but cannot face our Lord. I cannot tell him what I have done.

—My child, that is the mystery of confession, to unburden and leave it to him to carry the load.

—The confession booth is not wide enough to hold my sins. It is but a small boat in the center of a terrible sea.

Eugenia sat on a bench in the park across from the chapel. She bent over and tied her shoe. Earlier she had wrapped the money from the valise of Alexander in heavy brown paper. It was a good sum. She walked to the post office several streets away. At the post office she was given a small sturdy box and she wrote the address from the envelope of Irina's letter and posted it.

On the morning of her seventeenth birthday, Eugenia took a folded letter from a small wooden box with a dragonfly painted on the lid. It was the letter her father had pinned to her blanket in early winter of 1941. She was barely a year old but he had already detected a brightness in her that shone far beyond the farmhouse, the flowers in the yard, even the beauty of his wife. Eugenia opened her heart to feel what he felt, the great shadow of Stalin's troops advancing. Even as flowers budded and burst, heralding the coming of an obscene and terrible spring. She did not need to read, as she knew every word by heart. But her eyes fell on his last words. The letter slipped from her hands. She did not reach to pick it up.

The qualities that will help you get through life you have received from me. The qualities that will make you welcomed in heaven from your mother.

Eugenia took her skates from the closet and walked to the pond. It was crisp and bright, a day full of promise. She stopped here and there along the way, absentmindedly picking up small stones, filling the deep pockets of her old coat, the one that had struck Him with its inefficiency against the cold weather. She approached the clearing. The same small grove of trees the same pond beneath the same sky.

The priest had been kind but could not draw her out. Instead she chose to tell her story in the greater church, the green cathedral that is nature. For nature too is holy, more holy than the icons, more holy then the relics of saints. These were dead things compared to the most insignificant living thing. The fox knows this, and the deer, and the pine.

I am Eugenia, she said, offering her confession, the voice-over of her young life. She began with her first sense of him, of the pleasure she felt in being observed and how it ignited her performance. She told of her happiness in receiving the coat and the warmth it provided and how she sold herself for a little sack of screws from a poet's rifle, driven as much by curiosity as desperation. She left nothing out and as she described her consuming desire for him, she sensed with horror that a craving was yet within her. She told of washing his blood from her ankles, burying him without a single tear. As she relived that moment she wept at last, not for the loss of him but of innocence.

Eugenia carefully tied the laces of her skates. As she touched down upon the ice she felt a wholeness that had been so long absent. Everything came back to her swiftly and she performed with a harmony only silence could match. The animals in the forest gathered. A fox, a deer, a rabbit in the leaves. The birds appeared to be transfixed, perched upon the limbs of bordering trees.

The sun spread its warmth, signaling an early spring. The friction of her skates accelerated an already premature weakening of the pond's surface, precariously veined beneath a dangerously transparent layer. She did not slow down but whirled as if in the center of an infinity of infinities. That infamous space conjured and inhabited by mystics who no longer seek the nourishment of this earth. Free of all expectation or desire, she spun, and was at once the loom, the thread, the strand of gold. She bowed her head and lifted one arm toward the sky, surrendering, drawn by the gloved hand of her own conscience.

THE WHITENESS OF WINTER

Siberian Flowers

Siberian flowers are pink
as a daughter's circlet
a pale dressing gown
dragged across a window
not seen through again
There is blood everywhere
drained of its blood color
And the face of love is nothing
but the whiteness of winter
blanketing the hill
the fir and the pine
the fawn and the horn
Everything is blown
And yet we long
Two dark eyes
One head bowed
One fallen crown

A Dream Is Not a Dream

A FATHER'S DOOR

Light spreads across a desk fitted with an ashtray, pen, and a stack of foolscap. The writer hunches over and picks up the pen, thus leaving the world that flows beyond the heavy wooden door, carved with twin griffins, balancing a levitating crown. The room is still, yet the atmosphere is charged, a sense of horns locking.

Outside a young girl crouches beneath the foreboding herald, which seems to emit a soft reddish glow. She imagines she can hear the scratching of her father's pen. She waits furtively until it ceases to scratch, for then he will open the door, take her hand, descend the stairs and make her chocolate.

Why is one compelled to write? To set oneself apart, cocooned, rapt in solitude, despite the wants of others. Virginia Woolf had her room. Proust his shuttered windows. Marguerite Duras her muted house. Dylan Thomas his modest shed. All seeking an emptiness to imbue with words. The words that will penetrate virgin territory, crack unclaimed combinations, articulate the infinite. The words that formed *Lolita*, *The Lover*, *Our Lady of the Flowers*.

There are stacks of notebooks that speak of years of aborted efforts, deflated euphoria, a relentless pacing of the boards. We must write, engaging in a myriad of struggles, as if breaking in a willful foal. We must write, but not without consistent effort and a measure of sacrifice: to channel the future, to revisit childhood, and to rein in the follies and horrors of the imagination for a pulsating race of readers.

When I was yet in Paris I received an invitation from Albert Camus's daughter Catherine, to visit the Camus family home in Lourmarin. I seldom visit people's homes, for despite the hospitality offered I often suffer a feeling of confinement or imagined pressure. Almost always I prefer the comfortable anonymity of a hotel. But in this case I accepted; the honor was mine. After taking leave of Simone I circled back to Paris, boarded a train to Aix-en-Provence, and was met by Catherine's assistant for the hour's drive to Lourmarin. Any trepidation I may have felt dissipated with his kindness and the warmth of their reception.

The ancient villa, where silkworms were once bred, had been acquired with Camus's Nobel Prize money, to be their home away from Paris. My small suitcase was brought to the room which had once been his. Gazing from the window it was easy to see what drew him here. The naked sun, olive groves, dry patches of land dotted with tangles of yellow wild flowers all seemed akin to the natural setting of his native Algeria.

His room was his sanctuary. It was here that he labored over his unfinished masterwork *The First Man,* unearthing his ancestors, reclaiming his personal genesis. He wrote undisturbed, behind the heavy wooden door, carved with twin griffins supporting a crown. I could well imagine young Catherine tracing their wings with her finger, desiring nothing more than for her papa to open it.

I was fourteen when Camus lost his life in a fatal car crash. In the news that followed were pictures of his children, and a description of his valise, found in a field in the rain at the scene, containing his last manuscript. It was a humbling

VIEW OF LOURMARIN

experience to occupy, even briefly, the room where he had written it.

Modestly furnished, there were shelves lined with a range of his books. The three-volume set of *Journals de Eugène Delacroix*. *Lettres de Gauguin*. *La Vie de Mahomet*. *Le Viol des foules*, Serge Tchakhotine's chillingly relevant appraisal of the abuse of the masses through political propaganda. Before heading downstairs I returned to the window. Somewhere across the field, beyond the cypress trees, one may enter the cemetery where he rests aside his wife, his name somewhat eroded, as if nature had written a story of her own.

Catherine made lunch for us and prepared a violet-colored tea, a medicinal for my chronic cough. The conversation was warm and natural without a moment's awkwardness. Afterward I joined Catherine's daughter for a long walk with the dogs through the adjoining fields. We spoke of the trees, identifying them — cypress, fir, pine, young olive trees, fig, cherry trees heavy with fruit, and a commanding Cedar of Lebanon. She plucked some cherries for us as the dogs romped happily ahead. Toward the end of our walk she handed me a slender stem capped with tiny yellow flowers, a wild thing with a wisp of a fragrance. It's called *immortelle*, she said.

When we returned, Catherine's assistant beckoned me to the downstairs office, where they work and perform official duties. It was modest and contained an air of tranquil productivity. He asked if I would like to see the manuscript; I was so astonished that I could hardly manage an answer.

I was asked to wash my hands, which I did with some solemnity.

Camus's daughter entered, placing the manuscript of *Le Premier Homme, The First Man,* on the desk before me and went and sat in a chair giving us distance enough so that I could feel alone with it. For the next hour I was privileged to examine the entire manuscript page by page. It was in his hand, each page suggesting a sense of unflinching unity with his subject. One could not help but thank the gods for apportioning Camus with a righteous and judicious pen.

I turned each page carefully, marveling at the aesthetic beauty of each leaf. The first hundred watermarked sheets had Albert Camus engraved on the left-hand side; the remaining were not personalized, as though he had wearied of seeing his own name. Several pages were augmented with his confident marking, lines carefully revised and sections firmly crossed out. One could feel a sense of a focused mission and the racing heart propelling the last words of the final paragraph, the last he was to write.

I was indebted to Catherine for allowing me to examine her father's manuscript, primed to embrace this precious time, wanting for nothing. But slowly I discerned a familiar shift in my concentration. That compulsion that prohibits me from completely surrendering to a work of art, drawing me from the halls of a favored museum to my own drafting table. Pressing me to close *Songs of Innocence* in order to experience, as Blake, a glimpse of the divine that may also become a poem.

That is the decisive power of a singular work: a call to action. And I, time and again, am overcome with the hubris to believe I can answer that call.

The words before me were elegant, blistering. My hands vibrated. Infused with confidence, I had the urge to bolt, mount the stairs, close the heavy door that had been his, sit before my own stack of foolscap, and begin at my own beginning. An act of guiltless sacrilege.

I rested my fingertips on the edge of the last page. Catherine and I looked at one another, not saying a word. I handed her the manuscript, harboring a regret reserved for the end of an affair. I rose from the table, the unfinished violet tea gone cold, the immortelle left behind.

Wandering into the small town, I picture Camus rising from his desk, reluctantly setting his work aside. Observed by the ghost of a girl, he descends the stair, follows this same route, past the clock tower with the Latin inscription: *The hours that pass devour us.* He walks these same narrow cobblestone streets, taking his usual seat at Café de l'Ormeau. He lights a cigarette and has a coffee, surrendering to the village hum. In the distance lavender hills, almond trees, blue Algerian sky. Inevitably his mind will turn from the spur of amiable conversation back to his sanctuary, to a certain phrase that has yet to be resolved.

Things are slow moving. There is a pencil stub in my pocket.

What is the task? To compose a work that communicates on several levels, as in a parable, devoid of the stain of cleverness.

What is the dream? To write something fine, that would be better than I am, and that would justify my trials and indiscretions. To offer proof, through a scramble of words, that God exists.

Why do I write? My finger, as a stylus, traces the question in the blank air. A familiar riddle posed since youth, withdrawing from play, comrades and the valley of love, girded with words, a beat outside.

Why do we write? A chorus erupts.

Because we cannot simply live.

Written on a Train

MANUSCRIPT, LALANNE DESK, NEW YORK

Lim

He first noticed her on the street. He
noticed because she was heading the
opposite way from the other students
hurrying to school. She was small
with a determined air and a shock of
dark hair cut severely. A little
Simone Weil he remembered thinking,
the little witch.

Where she was hurrying was to a small
grove of trees just a kilometer away, to a that
hid a small pond, completely frozen
over. She no longer reported to school
and no one seemed concerned. Her aunt,
her teachers, whom she made uncomfortable
with her silence punctuated by startling
observations, including a stinging critique
of the teachers presentations.

A day without that girls piercing
stares, and rude sporadic comments
was a day of respite. She had no
particular friends and her aunt who

was responsible for her, was barely
responsible to her own self. often
missing for days in a lost in
a half remembered descent into
men + alcohol.

iced
The pond was uneven, her skate a
size too big, stuffed with crushed
news.
paper.

their handicaps surmounting
perhaps attributed to her style.
flawless jumps, a touchingly poetic
sensibility balanced a sense of
teetering, even danger as she flung
herself into space, an arm raised
above her. like a deranged top
negotiating a liquid ye amid
space, a few pines in the distance,
a bruised sky.

She skated for those same trees, that
same sky. No one saw her nor encouraged
or taught her. She was her own invention.
Seeing glimpses of skaters on the news,
on televised tournaments. which she
devoured for even a the nourishment
of love,

She could not remember when she was
first conscious of another presence,
at first a twinge of fear, which
melted as she mounted the ice.
as she ~~been in half and de~~ ~~spun~~
descending and ascending spirals.

The presence of him, another,
energized her performance, triggered
a vague competitive force she was
unaware existed, a muscle of
discontent flowing pride,
even showing off like
~~the~~ little star she
was consciously becoming.

He had followed her one morning on
a whim, watching her, hidden among
the trees. Her solo performance
so fully engaged, unique,
frightening. excited him,
a man of unusual control, solitary,
a trader of rare artifact, and
sometime arms, yet possessing

a rare sensitivity. To the object
he tracked down, delivered to
museums, sometimes kept near
in his modest yet exquisite
apartment with a balcony
overlooking the rooftops
of _____.

An unusual man, hidden in the
trees, as the weeks went by, in the
coldest winter on record. One morning
he did not appear but a box
was waiting by the edge of the
pond.

She instinctively knew it
was for her, from him. She removed
the few heavy rocks that kept
it stationary and opened it
slowly, trembling with a
a female excitement.
it was a coat, with the lined
impression of elegance, the of a
a delay fur that warmed her
before she slipped it on.
She looked around, toward his usual

spot. But there was no sense of
him. Perhaps he is saying goodbye
she thought, regretting she
had never given him as much
as a small wave of recognition

She pulled the collar to her, it was
a modest coat, cut simply, old fashion, a dark
mauve but the fit ~~was a~~
miracle, and the warmth was
the fit, the warmth a miracle.

princess style (research). •

That morning she did not skate,
~~filled with~~ stricken a banquet of confusion
the pleasure of receiving a gift,
that was designed solely for her.
The suspicious joy ~~she~~ that she felt,
the melancholy a taste of
joy that extended beyond her
solitude on skates, through her.

She felt a delight yet a fear of this
delight. for it seemed to eclipse

Even for a few brief hours, the
her desire to address the pond,
with courage and a prayer
and even a refreshing
hubris before she
made her first
mystically awkward
turn

There was a shift in the weather.
It was still very cold, but with
her coat, and a happy absence of
wind it felt as if a heat of
spring arrived.

She dreaded spring. for she had
no recourse reconsider but the
secret pond, and when the sun
replaced the blues of winter,
her & life on the ice would be
over.

HEADSTONE, SÈTE, FRANCE

filling the deep pockets ~~of the coat~~
~~with the fur lining. Her first gift~~
~~Such a warm coat was unnecessary~~
her old coat, dishinished cloth, that
had touched her benefactor with
its simplicity and inefficiency against
the ~~horrible~~ cold weather.

She removed her shoes and slipped on
her skates. As she touched down upon
the ice she felt the wholeness that
was absent, even in prayer. Everything
came back to her, every move, sense
of time, courage. She performed with
a harmony once silence could match.
The animals in the forest seemed to
gather. a fox, a rabbit on the leaves.
The birds, transfixed upon the limbs of
bordering trees.

The sun spread its warmth, a vengeance
of the coming spring. no longer content
to wait, the ice veining, a universe of
veins, ~~dis sessoring~~ the solidarity of
ice, melting at great speed.

due to the sun and the friction of
her skates, her motion, her speed.
She paid no heed, did not remove
her coat, heavy with stones,
but spun as if in the center
of an infinity of infinities:
the infamous space of
mystics who no
longer need
the nourishment
of the world
of the earth.
she spun
and was at once
the loom, the
thread the
strand
of gold
one
with heaven
and the depths
of unto
as if   which she
was drawn,
My the gloved hand of a
her own conscience

The author wishes to express gratitude to
The Albert Camus family
John Donatich
Dan Heaton   Christina Coffin
Alexandre Alajbegovic   Claude Lalanne
Fred Kameny   Laitsz Ho   Ariel Garcia
Rosemary Carroll
Andi Ostrowe   12 Chairs Cafe   Lenny Kaye

Photographs: Patti Smith,
Steven Sebring (pages 4, 96), Linda Bianucci (page 21)